A Mutt called Bo

Names: Watermeyer, Sean, Author
and Williams, Vanessa, Illustrator
Title: A Mutt called Bo / by Sean Watermeyer

Description: Cardiff: SABGE Publishing, [2020]
ISBN: 978-1-9161755-8-7

Subjects: Dogs, friendship, generosity

Manufactured in the UK
Written by Sean Watermeyer
and Illustrated by Vanessa Williams

Written by Sean Watermeyer

Illustrated by Vanessa Williams

In a beautiful park, in the shade of the trees
Children were playing as busy as bees.

A little bridge crossed a fast-flowing stream
And the children played Poohsticks
To laughter and screams.

By the side of that bridge sat a little boy
called Fred
Who sat crying quietly, his heart full of dread.

For Freddie had no friends of his own
to play
But this was to change on that very same day.

For today as Freddie sat alone in the park
From somewhere behind him he heard a dog
bark.

The little boy turned and was happy to see
A scruffy little dog as cute as can be.

The little dog came and sat down by his shoe
Titled his head and then said…

"How do you do?"

Freddie was amazed he couldn't believe it was true
He whispered…

**"Did you just speak,
was that just you?"**

The little dog nodded
Then did another amazing thing…

Looking up at the boy, he started to sing!

Songs of laughter to lighten your day
Songs to make you shout out

"Hip, Hip, Hurray!"

Then the little dog stopped singing
and looked up at Fred

"I know I'm just a dog but.."
He quietly said…

"But please will you come and play with me,
At least until it's time to go home for tea?"

Said Fred to the Mutt,
"You can talk and sing…
Wow! I bet you can do most anything!"

Of course we can play…

We can hop….

We can run…

"I'll be your friend and we'll have lots of fun!"

Freddie was so happy, his heart missed
a beat
With his new little friend, sat down by
his feet.

"If you don't mind me
saying, you are good mannered and tame
Please tell me little dog,
what is your name?"

"My name is 'Bo',
Now please throw me a stick,
I can run ever so fast, I'm ever so quick!"

So they ran, and they laughed with
wonderful play
Best friends they became on that warm
summer's day.

Then Freddie
found out, and let
the truth prevail…

His new friend had an extendable tail!

Not only could Bo talk,
And had wonderful songs
to sing
But his tail was like a
lasso,
It was a wonderful thing!

As the day passed by what a wonderful time they had,
It made Freddie so happy, and Bo so glad.

But then the thunder clouds gathered and there was no-
one around
And the raindrops came down with a 'pitter patter'
sound.

So under the bridge the two of them dashed
As the thunder roared and the lightening flashed.

The rain poured down from the dark angry sky
And the stream became a river, roaring on by.

So the boy and the dog
sheltered under the bridge.

But the river rose right up
Right up to the ridge!

And then they heard it,
a cry for help in the rain…
The voice they heard
Was clearly in pain!

Under the bridge and across the water
Was a little girl, her mother's daughter.

She was in the river holding onto a log
And her mother cried out
To the boy and the dog.

**"Help me please, my child
is in the river!"**

And down their spines
They felt a terrible shiver.

So as quick as a flash, they ran over the bridge
To the crying mother on the other side of the
ridge.

Then Bo said to Fred…

"Hold onto my tail!"

And he jumped into the river in the *howling* gale.

The little dog swam with all of his might
And his extendable tail was an amazing sight!

He swam and he swam, that brave little dog
Until finally he reached the girl on the log

To the little girl's surprise the brave Bo said…

**"Put your arms around my neck,
Your chin on my head."**

Then to the boy he shouted…

"Quick, pull us in!"

And Fred pulled his tail
With a smile and a grin.

So Freddie reeled them in
The little girl and the dog,
Brought them to safety
Through the rain and the fog.

And into her mother's arms…

Safe and *Tight*

It really was a wonderful sight.

They were then so happy
That they danced and they jived
For the little girl
Was both safe and alive!

But by now it was dark for time had passed,
And they all turned to Bo and gently asked…

"Bo, who is your owner and where is your house?"

And Bo went all sad and quiet as a mouse.
For he had no family
No place to go...

There was no home for the little dog called Bo…

Now Freddie's dad
Had been out looking for his boy,
He had been so worried
But now was full of pride and joy.

For he had seen his son
with a cute little dog,
As they rescued a girl
floating downstream on a log.

So he hugged his son,
and to the little Mutt said…

"You are one cool dog, and friend to my Fred…

But mostly you are kind
With the bravest heart,
With an amazing tale
And that's just a start!"

So Bo…

No more the empty streets and parks
You will roam…

**Now you are *family*,
Now you've a home!**

Printed in Great Britain
by Amazon